MAGGIE THE BAG LADY

Life as she lived it.
Life as she sees it.

by

Virginia Nygard

MAGGIE THE BAG LADY
Life as she lived it.
Life as she sees it.

Copyright 2020 by Virginia Nygard

Digital Formatting
by
Pamela Frost
Scatteredfrost Publishing
Cover art
Original watercolor by Scatteredfrost

www.scatteredfrost.com

ISBN-9798675317691

THIS BOOK BELONGS TO:

Margaret Mary Owl Byrd

This here's my friend
my companion
my sanity keeper

what sanity there is left.

I keep these notes so I remember
where I was
who I was
who I am
what I done
what I didn't
what to forget about
what's important
what to look forward to

if tomorrow comes.

So
this
is me.

If you find this, please tell my story to the world.

ACKNOWLEDGEMENTS:

My gratitude to the Florida Writers Association's Treasure Coast
Writers Group
and others for their perceptive evaluations, critique, and editing.

Also to Pamela Frost of Scatteredfrost Publishing
for her artistic portrayal of Maggie
and for her invaluable publishing expertise.

DEDICATION:

For all the Maggies and men of the world who share a version of her
story.
May they become visible to all as our sisters and brothers.

And, as always
for Walter, my soulmate.

TABLE OF CONTENTS

FOREWORD

When my husband and I lived in Boynton Beach, Florida, I worked at the West Palm Beach Public Library. That daily I-95 traffic was a grind.

To start the day with a little peace of mind, I left home early so I could stop and relax at a McDonald's near the library. Sometimes just for coffee, but often "coffee and" because there was always someone who could benefit from sharing the "and."

An assortment of early birds came from working folk and non-working folk, that is, those homeless who had survived another night on the streets. We talked and shared food and stories, and I came to know some very dear, very kind human beings in tough circumstances, often not of their own making.

Some of "Maggie's Memories" are woven from threads of their stories, and those of others. Some are uniquely Maggie's whose voice rises from the empathy I share with fellow human beings.

We are all ONE.

"Whoever oppresses a poor man insults his Maker,
but he who is generous to the needy honors him."
Proverbs 14:31 ESV

GRACE

I tire of those looks
when some people see me
pushing my cart.

You know.
The side-eyed, don't-quite-see-you,
There, but for the grace of God, go I
looks.

Well, how I feel about that is,
when God was passing out *race*
I thought he said *grace*
and I said, "Gimme all y'got."

So he did.

Just about.

Miccosukee, Black, and Irish.

Maybe more I'll never know.

Like Chinese.

Or Eskimo.

Which ain't all that bad, y'know?

Because that way,

I come able to see people

the way they be.

Which is

just like me.

Inside.

And maybe that ability

is the grace

those poor folk

don't have.

And there's the pity.

MAGIC WAND

When I was seven and crying
Mama hushed me
saying
there was a magic wand for everything
like changing tears to smiles.

Like Daddy gone away?
Can it bring him back?

My older brothers
      Sam and Adam
scolded Mama.
What you tellin' her lies for?
Ain't no magic wand nowhere!

But I looked in Mama's warm, gold eyes
and saw no lies there.
I saw what I wanted to see.

Comfort.
Not the hard years to come
when day after day
that magic wand of Mama's
only took good things away,

and never brought them back.

Most everything I believed in
swept out of my life
like puffs of dust
when you shake a rug.

First Daddy
    then the Tooth Fairy
        then the Easter Bunny.
And when Santa Claus drifted away
    I wondered if Jesus
        would stay.

⌘   ⌘   ⌘

BROTHERS TO THE END— ALMOST

When we was kids in West Palm

all our yards had plank fences

old as our shotgun houses

       but in worse shape.

Still, like good referees

they kept kids and cats and dogs where they belonged.

       Mostly.

While me and my girlfriends jumped rope in the yard

Sam and Adam, and Elijah

       their partner in crime

jumped and scrapped like junkyard dogs

yowlin' and itchin' for mischief.

       That set General Sherman

—the old brindled bulldog next door—

to growling and howling his own discontent

like he was declaring war!

Now. Back then, my mama sometimes said

When God in heaven was giving out brains,

Elijah and your brothers thought He said trains—

and they surely missed theirs!

Mama was right again.

They took the General's challenge.

We girls thought the bulldog's battle cry

was going to be his last

because these boys aimed to make that dog

their *goat* for the day!

One loose plank

hung from the fence crossbar

by one old nail

like a loose tooth

wiggling free of its kin.

Sam and Elijah and Adam swung that plank aside

and broke out of their backyard jail

into mighty high adventure.

They ran circles around the General

barking and howling their own selves

laughing and pointing at his stubby legs

so bad the old dog couldn't catch them.

Well.
General Sherman, he stopped
        drew in second wind
                and
charged and jumped 'round them bug-eyed boys
        a-snarling and snapping his toothy old grin
nipping at butts and ankles and legs.
        The battle had turned!

The boys high-tailed it back
to that loose-tooth doorway to home.
Long-legged Sam and Elijah
flew through the hole so fast
the plank
swung—and—swung—and— *Bam!*
It
        stuck
                shut.

Last comes little Adam
but the plank won't budge and General Sherman's charging full on.

Adam's yanking the plank and yelling for help

—half a lifetime to hear him say later—

his voice shooting higher

      his eyes growing wider

in fear he'd be gulped down

      pants—and—all!

But Sam and Elijah pried at the plank

till it slipped aside loose

just in time.

The fence gulped Adam down

and slammed shut again.

     Bam!

So General Sherman

he mumbled off

in a satisfied huff

ready for another Atlanta.

Now, many boys are like untrained pups

caterwauling and brawling

to be King of the Hill.

But free of a tug on the leash
            sometimes
they end up just like old dogs
—ignored—or beaten—or bruised—
            or abused by the way of the world.
                  You hear?

What goes around comes around.
            So
you pups mind every step.
Ask yourself
            How would I feel if that dog was me?

            And that's a true tale
            I told three young boys

teasing a skinny old black dog
            tied to a scrawny old pine tree
                  in the park
                        yesterday

REMEMBERING T.J.

Hot day for April.

I'm biding time

watching squirrels and birds and lizards

scratch out a living in the park.

White City Park

where few white folk gather now.

Some kinda look at me

like I don't belong

but I do.

I belong everywhere.

I be part Miccosukee

part white

part black

maybe more than that.
So I fit in wherever I be
and wherever I be
some always think I don't belong.
I see it in their eyes.

Sitting here in shelter shade
memories of my daddy
rise from still, dark water.
He was broody, still, and dark, too.
Thomas Jefferson Blue Byrd
born April Fool's Day, nineteen-thirty
and the joke was on him.
He was born near black as coal
and never could figure why
no Jefferson white lightened his skin.
Skipped a generation or so, I guess.

T. J., my daddy, carried scars inside
that tied his life in knots of sorrow.
He coulda been a real good man
but hard, early lessons lived on
taught him places he didn't belong

like watching his Papa Joe

be strung up

and hung up on an old oak tree

for dallying with a white whore

in Greengallows

South Carolina

September 18, 1937.

Lesson: A white whore is white first.

The noun don't matter.

The adjective do.

T.J. was seven years old.

Sleep in peace, Daddy.

We carry on remembering.

You were wronged.

You always belonged.

And so do I.

So do we.

Right here in White City Park.

⌘　　⌘　　⌘

VISIBILITY CHARM

Funny thing happened today.

Most people don't see me, y'know?

To my surprise, somebody did.

A pretty young thing with honest eyes.

I was sitting in Burger King

chomping on fries and a burger.

She smiled and pushed my cart aside.

Mind if I sit? Mind if we chat?

Suit yourself, I said. I squirted more ketchup on my fries.

You live around here?

I live everywhere.

I'm Kathy, she said.

Maggie.

Maggie what?

I swallowed my fries and my pride.
They call me Maggie the Hag
or Maggoty Mag.
I'm not maggoty. I clean up.
Sometimes at the library.
Sometimes at the shelter.
It's just
some mean folks call me that.
They gotta be mean
'cause somebody's done the same to them
time and again
and maybe worse.
Back of the anger in their eyes
prickling pain sets the mean a-fire.
They gotta feel somebody's worse off than them
so they take it out on me.
Let it be, my Mama would say, so I do.

Well, Miz Kathy, nice meeting you.

Thanks for the chat and the smile.

You made Invisible Maggie visible

> for a while.

Maybe

> I'll see you again?

HANDICAPPED

The library inside is quiet and cool.

Outside, July—the fool—screams *I'm here, Florida!*

 Like we don't know it.

 Not even noon and I stink.

The clerk eyes my shopping bag.

I smile back and pull on the ladies' room door.

The handicap stall's my private bathroom.

 Without a tub.

 So I make do.

I strip buck naked, hang it all on the hook.

 Hang your clothes on a hickory limb

 but don't go near the water.

 No problem, Mama. I'll make do.

With wet paper towels and sweet soap

I proceed to scrub me up.

God, it's good to wash my privates!

>   I put on fresh clothes out my shopping bag.

        Feel almost human.

Two females come in chattering and clattering like magpies.

One must be on a walker or—yup—a wheelchair.

See it there under the door.

You almost done in there? We need that stall!

I dump my stinking clothes in the sink

rinse and wring them quick

pack them back in a plastic bag

and make my exit fast as I can.

Some nerve! You don't belong in that stall.
You're not handicapped at all!

Yes, ma'am

        in a different way I am.

You ladies have a blessed day.

REFLECTION IN A BMW

Young gal slides out her car eyeing me with scorn

oozing

like pus from the sores on my privates.

Like she's gonna catch something just by looking at me.

Pretty bitch in her sparkling spike heels

plumping her ass up for horny eyes.

That handkerchief skirt don't cover much.

They seeing plenty and wanting more.

Jewelry jangling head-to-toe...*Look at me!*

Fancy nails and painted face.

Gilding the lily, Mama always said.

She's gonna catch something all right.

But not from me.

Sugar, that BMW of yours don't make you no better

than me with my shopping cart.

Just richer.

And I oughta know.

You're like looking in my mirror thirty years back.

Wish I knew then

what I know now.

Good luck, Sugar.

DEALING WITH THE HELP

Finally got me a clinic appointment.

I hate going like

I hate old Satan himself.

Reason One:

It ain't no fun.

Have to bury my cart in my secret place

under scruffy brush and dry leaves

where we sleep.

Sadie, me, and another lady

    Madge, I think.

We three agree to watch out for each other.

Got much the same in our bags and carts

                    so
since nothing from nothing is nothing
stealing ain't worth
losing someone who cares
                    except
if we get any money
it's stuffed in our bras and socks.

Reason Two:
There's no safe, close place
to make a bed and lay my head
the night before I go.
So there's three morning miles to cover
for the free shuttle
down at the bus depot door.
Gotta be waiting by eight a.m.
to save walking five miles more.

Reason Three:
The woman at the clinic desk.
She looks at me like she sees right through
                    and nothing feels worse.

Except maybe

nightmares

　　　and noises

that scare me awake.

I crave for somebody who looks deep

beneath my rags, my withered skin

to see my soul, know who I am

　　　the me I haven't been since I was ten.

　　　Watch out what you wish for!

　　　The doctor looked under my rags, all right.

　　　Saw a pitiful sight, I know.

　　　Still, he spoke soft, like I was somebody

　　　while he cleaned out the sores

　　　and soon said I'd be good as new.

I said

Since I've been around a long time

good-as-new just ain't gonna do.

Can't you make me better than new?

He patted my hand, said I'd be fine

'cause *better-than-new* would take a long time.

The doctor and I shared a laugh at that,

and the nurse even managed a smile.

So I left feeling better for knowing

      in time I'll be fine.

⌘   ⌘   ⌘

PSALM 58:1

Mama read me the Bible.

And I been through enough to know she was right.

She said when it came down to it

it don't matter if they're judges or juries

politicians or pastors.

Like anybody else, they're human

good, bad, or between hell and heaven.

Their vices can bloom in daytime

beneath the shade of power

or by the dim light of the moon.

They might shed their clothes
to indulge in perversion
            or pay the prostitute's price.
And then by morning's light
they slip on their robes and follow
            to   the   letter
            of their laws and codes
and make value judgments
            on vulnerable souls.

Amen, Mama.

And I could name names.

LOOKIN' BACK

April. I love it. Perfect Florida day.

Warm sun. Cool air.

Got a bench to myself at Riverwalk

down off Veteran's Memorial Parkway.

I see a daddy and his two boys

come by, set up fishing poles.

Faces shining, they talking, laughing

like daddies and little boys should.

I dig down in my cart.
Take Mama's tin sewing box
out its plastic bag.
Finger the picture on the lid
      a mama sitting and sewing
      with her little girl and two boys
      at her knee.
When I was little, I named them
for me and my brothers.
Margaret Mary Owl Byrd
      Samuel Strong Byrd
         Adam Angel Byrd.

Inside I find our pictures,
faded now by age and time.
Just like me.

There's Daddy with Sam and Adam,
just eight and seven
at the north fork of the St. Lucie River
learning how to bait a hook.
Brings tears to my eyes.

Daddy gone a year later.

And this one is my Mama
and me, just six
hugging and smiling
like all's right with the world.
But it wasn't.

Daddy gone a year later.

I look up and see
that daddy and his boys
still talking and laughing
like daddies and little boys should.

Lord willing, they stay that way
to the end of their days.

MONSTERS

October.

Nice weather.

Drying out.

Cooling down.

For the most part.

Florida starting to make sense

as a place to live.

Then October roars out

with Halloween.

All Hallows brings out

Innocence and Evil

kids that play at spooking

and freaks who get kicks from doing

unspeakable things to creatures

big and small

old and young

and helpless.

Daddy always told us

there was enough evil in the world

without us adding to it.

His eyes always held that faraway look

seeing himself watch Papa Joe die

at the hands of freaks

September 18, 1937.

And it wasn't even Halloween.

⌘　⌘　⌘

THE PRINCE FROG

Mary Deer Kawayi

my mama

     both white and Miccosukee

fell for the spell

of the dark

Thomas Jefferson Blue Byrd.

     Negro

polite folk called him back then.

Me, I was blinded by the light.

Flaming red hair

     sea-green eyes

        of a charming Scot.

Aleck Adair Webster.

He told me about his fancy names.
Our people and names are Scottish, he said.
While Scotch is a very fine whiskey!
      So
Aleck   meant defender of mankind
Adair   meant beautiful
Webster   was the word for weaver.
He played the game so sweet
he whisked me off my feet
when I was nineteen.
      And we flew away on wings of love
      to the Carolina piney woods
      where nothing stood but a shabby cabin
      on land his granddaddy once owned.

There our twin babies
soon were born
near midnight so close
each got his own birthday
      one the fourteenth
      one the fifteenth
      of February
      1978.

Aleck's little joke

was their twin names

> Todd and Fox

'cause where his granddaddy came from

> Todd means Fox.

Wasn't long after

Aleck turned out to be

> no defender of his family

> not so beautiful

but a good weaver

> of lies and deceptions.

My Scottish Prince

turned out to be nothin' more

> than an enchanting frog

who sent me to turn tricks

> into money

> to feed us.

OVER A BARREL

Two banker types, grinnin'
and crowin' over some big deal
cigar smoke drifting by their heads
pushed by me on the sidewalk.

We got him over a barrel, said the older.
The young'un laughed. *We sure did!*

    Wasn't so much the glee that got me
    as *over a barrel* did.

I remember the time when I was nine
and we lived on a West Palm Beach hill
(just a bump in the road to some)
Sam and Adam and their pals
         skated fancy figure eights
in the middle of the street
         trying to dazzle us gals.

The big boys tipped a barrel over
and dared each the other to jump it.
         Mighty fine acrobats they were,
skimming the barrel and skating away
         or flopping kerplop on their butts
until it came to Adam.

The littlest one wouldn't be outdone.
He screwed up his courage and jumped.
Shy of clearing the edge by an inch
         his skate clipped the rim
the barrel upended and Adam fell in.
         Feet first!

Of course, it fell over and rolled down the hill
with Adam inside, yellin' for Jesus
to save his young life.

When our screams broke the spell,
    the boys scrambled like hell
    a-shouting and waving cars off at crossroads
        till the barrel stopped dead
          in a field.
Well.
Them boys was scared near white with fear
till Adam popped out with a big silly grin
saying
That was such fun, Let's do it again!

Now, about that poor man
barrel-rolled by the bankers

I sure hope he has a good trick or two
hiding up in his own business sleeve
so he can pop up with a big grin and say
    This was fun, gentlemen!
    Let's do business again.

               ❧ ☙

LESS THAN A WOODEN INDIAN

Thank God for Mr. Smelt's Smoke Shop.

Going to set awhile here on the iron bench next to Tonto.

He's the wooden Indian who sets here

day and night

day in, day out

trying to sell a fistful of wooden cigars.

Business not so good, eh, Tonto?

Still, you ain't been fired for setting down on the job!

And you don't hurt.

No brain, no pain, right?

Now, me—my feet and hips hurt so bad

they ache like remembered sorrows that make me cry.

These Goodwill shoes don't help, neither.

Reminds me of TJ, my daddy

seven years old in the orphanage.

Headmistress said the *state spies* were coming to visit.

TJ got sent to town to buy a pair of second-hand shoes.

Afraid of getting a beating for failing

he bought the only pair in the old shop

women's shoes.

Daddy always laughed when he told that story.

Us kids always felt sad.

He never said what the old witch at the orphanage did

when she saw women's shoes.

Sure would like to seen her face.

All's I know is Daddy survived.

Thank y' Lord.

Mr. Smelt just slipped me a fiver to move on.

Seems I don't help the shop's image much.

Tonto does better as a solo act.

The wooden Indian's assistant just got fired.

Adios, Kimosabe.

RAIN

Okay.

Must be somebody up there now

in those rainclouds

apologizing for Florida being desert-dry

and bursting out in grass fires

for the past six months.

Hey.

Yeah, July be part of rainy season,

but you don't have to send a monsoon!

Makes me think about getting pontoons

to slide around on in Fort Pierce.

Rain?

I'm talkin' sheets of rain.

Big—gray—sheets.

Not dainty-lace-hankies-of-rain.

Not middlin' pillowcases of rain.

But whole—damn—gray—sheets—of rain.

Ain't there somebody else on earth

who's worth sharing Your water with?

Well.

Anyway.

Thank You.

And that nice Salvation Army lady

     who has You in her heart

for this hand-me-down slicker I got.

     Lady's name is Lillian.

Whenever I stop by

she shares cookies she baked,

cold water and soda in summer

hot coffee when it's

     hardly what Yankees call *winter*

but cold just the same.

Lillian saw me shelter under their roof today

with a soppin' shawl 'round my head and shoulders

> when them sheets of Yours come smothering down.

> She come running out, asking me in.

And, praise be, I come out

hand-me-down new and dry

with a bright yellow slicker

and hoodie to boot.

> Oh, yeah, and boots, too.

When I asked her why, Miss Lillian said

> *My library friend says*

> *when you edit the Bible to basics*

> *it comes down to*

> *"Do unto others as you*

> *would have them do*

> *unto you."*

And that's all there is to it!

"Down these mean streets a man must go who is not himself mean."
- Raymond Chandler

WARRIOR

The years hung heavy

on his chiseled face

worn, but proud.

    And around it

    was dreads

    thinning

    growing gray.

But the light

in his eyes

shone warm and strong.

    I could tell the tribe within his race

        Masai!

    Warrior to the end.

At Route One and the Boulevard

he held a card that said

SEE ME.

I AM.

I WILL WORK FOR FOOD.

FEED ME.

I AM.

I WILL WORK FOR YOU.

And, bless my soul

I got chills all over remembering

one Sunday some time back

that newspaper girl, Kathy

    the one who saw me

    and fed me in Burger King one day

she took me to Unity

where I heard them say

    I AM

    is the name God calls himself.

Right that second

the Masai looked at me and smiled.

I turned and dug down in my cart
for Mama's sewing box.
Pulled out a crumpled dollar
smoothed it on my skirt
and walked to where he stood.

Name's Maggie, I said.
Somebody done me a good turn
and one deserves another, I said
handing him my shabby dollar.

Name's James, said he.
You did see me.
You did feed me.
And I
   will
     work for you.

❦ ❧

THAT GIRL

I'm sittin' in Burger King the other day

nursing a senior coffee refill

my cart tucked under plastic outside

waiting for the rain to go away.

When in comes that white girl.

She got green hair chopped short on the sides

purple and orange popped up on top.

       Eyes black as sin ringed round

       with.... Looks like coal tar.

She got earring hoops

a dog could jump through

      a tiny silver bone through her nose

      and lipstick purple as a summer night sky.

When she talks you can see a gold ball

bobbing up and down on her pierced tongue.

      How she eats anything I'll never know.

      How she blows her nose, I'll never know.

Where else she got pierced

I don't want to know.

      And why she done all that

      I'll never know.

Then I hear my mama say,

Margaret Mary Owl Byrd!

Somebody in here right now

is looking at you wondering how

you fell on hard times

and why you choose to live your life

the way you do.

Yes, Mama. Probably so.

And just then I see that girl
looking at me and coming my way.

She smiles, sets down a tray
piled high with a fine feast
and two Cokes.

"Hey, Maggie. I'm Faith.
Jeez, look at these eats.
I was born with eyes the size
        of my stomach.
I bought way too much.
        I always do.
Would you
        care to break bread with me?"

Yes, Mama, I know-
Never judge a book by its cover.

And I guess I'll find out
how she eats.

⌘   ⌘   ⌘

MANNA CAFÉ

Oh, Lord.

    Here she comes.

        Sister Sunshine.

In that big old white robe

and that big gold cross and chain

you know she's a tough boss

in spite of that hallelujah grin.

I can't help grinnin' back.

I'm thinkin'

She looks like Whoopie Goldberg in *Sister Act*.

    Only not as pretty.

Maggie! How you doin' today?

Fine, Sister, fine. Thank ya'.

Did you get enough to eat, girl?

Oh, yes, ma'am, I got enough, thank ya'.

(Canned corn, peas, Chef Boyardee, and Twinkies.
But like Mama always said
"Beggars can't be Choosers,
so you hush up and eat."
And I'll eat anything that ends with Twinkies.)

Can't I get you anything at all, Maggie? There's plenty.

(I know where this sweet talk's leading,

and I ain't having *none* of it.

I came here today to get away from bugs

and mosquitoes and egg-frying heat.

I also came to eat.

And Sister Sunshine knows

I didn't come to hear her pray and preach.

Maybe...I can get away...if...I just fib and say...)

No, no thank ya', ma'am, I'm fine.

Well, then, dear...let us bow in prayer.

(Oh, Lord!)

SKIN DEEP

Fourth of July.
Sometimes traveling light pays off.
Slept in a thicket by the pond
near the parade route.
Yesterday's egg sandwich
and a bottle of water
done me just fine for breakfast.

Got me a perfect perch
under a clump of shady trees
before all the white folk and their families
could claim it.

Like their kind done everything else.

Margaret Mary Owl Byrd!
Have you forgotten all I've taught you?
Judge not, lest ye be judged.
Do unto others....

Sorry, Mama. Kisses from my heart.
But you know as I do
all white folks ain't like you.

Oh, I see.
Just all of pure black and red and yellow blood
are perfect.

No, Mama, heart of mine,
with skin as fine as porcelain
like Daddy always said
there's good and bad in all.

But

things haven't changed from your day

and

You are beginning to get under

My skin

where *you* have never been.

Very well, my sweet, sad child,

go watch your parade.

Just remember how much love there was

for a child of another color

When I carried

you under my skin.

MEMORIES IN THE AIR

Saturday.

Food truck day at the Civic Center.

So Sadie, Madge and me

rummaged in our socks and bras

and came up with cash enough

to make our one meal count.

Smells of all that food

riding on the breeze

brought memories galloping in.

Sadie, eyes wide
like a little child
stared at candy apples
red and shiny
lined on a tray
like soldiers
waiting for battle.
Said they were her favorite treat
when summer fairs set up in her town.
May be why she lost so many teeth.
Sadie grins like a jack-o-lantern.

Funnel cakes frying put Madge in mind
of carnivals in New Jersey.
She loved them cakes buried
below sugar-powder mountains
deep enough to cover her nose.
A wonder she didn't choke.

My sweetest memory?
The circus rolling into Miami.
Daddy took our family to see
the circus train!

Oh, my!

Such glee to see elephants lumbering by

animal cages roll off cars painted in red and gold

like horse-drawn wagons of old.

Ringling Brothers it was.

The Greatest Show on Earth.

Not that I could say for sure.

We never had money for tickets.

But, oh, we'd come back

and stroll the whole sideshow

filling our little heads with memories.

Somehow, Mama and Daddy eked out

just enough money

to fill bellies with hot dogs, pop

and my favorite treat—cotton candy.

Pink.

Sam and Adam, of course, picked blue.

Said it wouldn't do for boys to pick pink.

Then grinning, and laughing
like circus clowns
free of woe, rich as kings
we all rode home with happy hearts.

Seeing what prices be here today
Sadie, Madge and me
settled for hot dogs
split a Coke.

Large.

And shared my cotton candy.

Pink.

⌘   ⌘   ⌘

THE LION

Parked my cart by McDonald's door.

Leon looked out the window. Nodded.

I knew he'd watch my cart.

He come to open the door.

Leon's a good man.

Not book smart

> or street smart

or otherwise

> but he's got

the kindest heart you'd ever meet.

I got us two double cheeseburgers.

Got Leon a cherry Coke.

Got me a sweet iced tea.

Nothing like the tea Mama used to make.

      Not as sweet or as strong.

Funny how little things

puts me in mind of Mama.

While we chaw down our burgers

Leon tells me again

      My name means lion

      'cause my mama knew I'd be strong and brave

      and if you're strong and brave

      you got a 'sponsibility to be kind and helpful

      so mama taught me to behave nice and smile

      and say please and thank you

      so thank you for the double cheeseburger

      and the Cherry Coke, Miss Maggie.

      I love Cherry Coke.

Then Leon the Lion chomps another big bite

grins and chaws at the same time.

Which ain't all that pretty.
But I sure ain't all that pretty either.
So I can't throw a stone at Leon.
But if pretty is as pretty does
Leon's goodness shining out
makes him pretty enough.

I think that's why McDonald's lets Leon
set at that tiny table by the door.
It puts me in mind an old-time school desk.
He helps folks with wheelchairs and walkers
and carries trays and never gets in the way.

Leon knows when enough is enough.
He's got a kind of animal sense about people.
More sense about people than some people have.

Maybe Leon got shorted on book smarts
but behind those coal-black eyes
he's plenty kind and wise.

I bet he'd like a vanilla cone.

SEEING EYE TO EYE

Went to the clinic

when the stye on my left eye felt like

a bumblebee made himself to home

and sat there

slowly

closing

that eye.

Weren't from vanity I saw the doc.

Got enough to worry about

keeping myself together

without being

a one-eyed bag lady.

While Doc fixed me up
I thought of my daddy
Thomas Jefferson Blue Byrd.

When T.J. was five
Papa Joe gave him a little hatchet
so he could play at chopping wood.
One day
not seeing T.J. tagging behind
Papa Joe swung his big ax
back over his head
and nicked T.J. right by his left eye.
Sliced the brow right through.

Papa Joe scooped up his boy and ran to the cabin.
Mama Bessie tore a piece of her petticoat
swiped cobwebs down from up in the corners
and wrapped the bandage
'round T.J.'s head.

Gave her brave wounded soldier

a long hug, his wooden musket

set him in his little rocking chair

and said he could guard the house from there.

Grandma Bessie

I know

and you know

what most people don't know

Life's chopped me up some

but my bandages don't show.

And

I could use a hug, too.

PUBLIX PARKING LOT

I ain't judging you
with your basket full of food
as you swing a wide circle around me.
I see your squinty eyes look at me sideways
like you wished I wasn't there.

Like that snake I crept up on once.
Only he had the decency to turn
and look me in the eye
before I bashed his brains out with a tree branch.

Hey!
Don't you be judging me
'cause that snake had it coming.

I made myself a nice bed of leaves under the trees
by the preserve.
Hidden real good.
Down by the culvert near the pond.
Covered the leaves with curtains out the Goodwill garbage.
Tucked them in real nice and tight.
A nice clean mattress.
Better than that buggy one in the last shelter I stayed.
Better out here on the streets.

Almost.

So don't you judge me like that damned snake.
He had the whole woods
and where did he take root?
Smack on top of my clean mattress.

Tell me you wouldn't take a tree branch to somebody broke in your
house.

⌘　⌘　⌘

FAITH HOPE FLOWERS

Picked up the Saint Lucie News Tribune
left behind on that table there.
      Read it front to back.
Mama used to say I read newsprint
clear off the paper.

I chewed on my Big Mac
and frontpage news too.
      Swallowed the good with the bad
      and felt kinda sick at my middle.
      Don't think I'll do that again!
I turned past ads for stuff I don't buy
and deep inside was a real happy sight.

Miss Faith Hope Flowers
who bought too much food
        on purpose
        one day at BK
and shared that feast with me.

That day, she shared more than food, too.

Said how her mom withered and died
from am-yo...am-yo...oh, you know.
        Lou Gehrig Disease.

Said her dad, broken hearted
        and just plain broke
made a grow house of their house
        and lost it.
He done time and become lost himself.

Then Faith's big sis, Charity Love, turned tricks
to feed the three of them.
She fought like hell with little Faith

      to *keep* the faith
      to stay in school and make her way
      no matter what anyone said.

      And Faith Hope did.
      She was one tough kid.

Her hair's grown out now, I see here.
Not green and purple and orange no more.
Slicked on back in a tight, brown ponytail.
Heh.
That silver bone in her nose is gone.
Heh.
Don't know what she done about the pierced tongue.

Oh, for sure, at the start she had a rebel heart
but it held no tolerance for hate.
      Her heart was open.
      Her heart was good.

I told her in time she would pick the right road.

So. You see here?
There stands Miss Faith Hope Flowers.
smiling at me like she's saying

See, Maggie?
Told you I'd get my nursing degree!
Thanks for keeping faith in me!

GREEN EYES

Sadie, Madge and me
sitting in the shade of a tree
outside McD's.
Just watching.

Of a sudden, Sadie says
Look there.
Ain't she the cutest little girl?
Caramel-colored hair
in natural corkscrews
that white gals have to buy.
Why, her bright face is light
as new potato skin
and speckled with freckles!

And those

wide

green

eyes

don't miss a trick!

Uh-huh, we three agree.

Madge now sees what I'm seeing

and she pipes up.

As sure as I'm sitting here

this child's got Irish in her.

Heh.

And not the Black Irish.

Pardon the joke, Maggie.

Look at her smile like a movie star!

See her strut her stuff for the big folks?

She already knows how to make

cuteness

pay off.

Uh-huh, we three agree

and they look at me.

So I say

Back in the day

when I had mighty fine stuff to strut

I shared a corner in Lauderdale

with a gal named Jezebel

corkscrew hair the color of caramel

new potato skin

and wide green eyes that didn't miss a trick.

Just like this child

Jezzie and I

knew how to make cuteness

pay off.

DUCKS OF A FEATHER

Some folks have empty hearts.

Oh, they go to church

every Sunday

but sit there with the preacher's words

sliding off their oily souls

like mallards paddlin' in the pond

rain rolling off their oily feathers.

Some can spout the Good Book

giving chapter and verse

keen at bending the meaning

when it suits their need.

But they don't do no good
for themselves
        or anybody else.
        And *ye shall know them by their deeds!*

At the shelter Wednesday afternoon,
when it was cold enough
to freeze the—tail—off a brass monkey
I wiped down tables, and half-watched
a rerun of an old western show on TV.
Of a sudden what one cowboy said
sounded like he read what's in my head:
        "The trouble is, we practice a lot of religion
                but not much Christianity."

And that's because
some folks have empty hearts.

⌘ ⌘ ⌘

GRANDMAS

I'm smiling and watching
a grandma like me
and her blond baby boy
sitting in the shade of palms
on a bench by the waterfront
in Fort Pierce.
Lunch bag and Cokes between them.
They laughing, loving time together
talking about animals they see in the clouds.

Puts me in mind of my daddy
and his mama, Bessie Byrd.
Now and again he'd tell a story
eyes glistening through love-and-loss tears
the kind that lived behind his eyes
and every single time came back
when a Grandma story came to mind.

Like the time food was scarce
and the bottom of the pot
came too soon.
Daddy and his Papa Joe
got the last of the squirrel stew.
Papa Joe needed strength to find work.
My daddy needed food to grow.
Bessie brewed tea from dried roots
and drank her supper.

Now, look at that lucky child over there
with a sandwich and Coke all his own.
Think I spy a chocolate chip cookie, too.
Blessings overflowing, bless his heart.

As that boy grows,
I hope life never shows him
the bottom of the pot.

SMART ALECK

I'm sitting out of the sun, resting my bones
on the bench outside Winn-Dixie
at Midway and Route One.

Here comes this young buck rankin' on his girl
how she's too dumb to hold a job
and she oughta do something with her scraggy hair
and get her nails done
and she can't even cook worth a shit.
All of which he could overlook
if she had enough by way of boobs and booty
to make a joyride worth his time.

Lord, this sends me back forty years

when I finally got the guts

to kick that worthless man out my life.

    Aleck Adair Webster.

Smart Aleck, they called him, and rightly so!

    A.A. they called him too

    and that's where he belonged

    Alcoholics Anonymous.

But he never had the guts.

So I got out before he hurt me worse.

Fresh out of insults, this boy stalks off.

The girl turns, tears blurring her eyes.

    Or maybe they're mine.

    Or both.

I know so well the pain his brutal words cause

    like an angry tomcat scratched them on her heart.

I'm thinking hard:

> *Baby, Baby, let him go.*
> *He ain't worth shit!*

> *I hope you know!*

Does she hear my thoughts?

She reaches for her phone

> walks off.

I guess I'll never know.

FLORIDA SEASONS AND ME

Some say there's only one season in Florida.

Nope.

There's four.
Just seems like one
because they have fun jumpin' around.
Those rebels don't stick to the calendar
like in most places.
Hereabouts, they make their own rules.
They play hide and seek in and out of months
messin' with everybody's minds.

Like

When we think Spring's here from March to May

There'll come a day when
steamy, stinky Summer sneaks in
reeking of sweat
blowing his hot, humid breath
like some old wino.

Or

Sometimes in Fall, as late as November
you think the steam bath's over
and you're gonna open your windows
hoping cool breezes blow through on ya'
like riding the Titanic
up front.

Nope.

Freezin' as Frosty the Snowman,
Ol' Man Winter slips out of the dark like a preemie
and you

shocked it ain't the date he's due

you gotta keep them windows shut!

That old devil will have *his* due.
He just don't tell nobody when.

Heh.

Don't matter to me and my shopping cart
how many seasons there be
or when.

Nope

We got no windows.

And the shelter got heat and AC.

⌘   ⌘   ⌘

MADGE'S GRANDBABY GIRL

Me and Madge was sitting out of the rain

jawing and catching our breath

on the benches out front of Publix

  when up comes the subject of death.

She sees a girl child, maybe sixteen

swole up with a babe in her belly

and Madge's eyes come awash with tears.

  When I asked why, she told me.

That child put her in mind of her grandbaby

Princess, the shining light of all their lives

who held the promise of a better future

        but fell to a wandering man's wicked wiles.

Only help she got from the preacher was scripture:

Before I formed you in the womb I knew you,

and before you were born, I consecrated you...

        and that God's child was not hers to undo.

I told Madge that my mama

read me the Bible through and through

and God meant those words for Jeremiah, the prophet

        not for a child done wrong to!

Don't matter none now, they're gone.

Princess and the little babe, too.

Maybe God took 'em back to fix a mistake

        or give Princess a new chance to choose.

GOOD MORNING?
HELL NO IT AIN'T!

I woke up this morning

somewhere under a clump of trees

because somebody was talking.

Turns out it was me.

The other me.

The me who scares away evil

with the switchblade I got in my pocket.

Shit, I hear her say, *We sure showed that knifebird, didn't we?*

Wasn't no knifebird.

I ain't *that* old he comes looking for me.

Well, whoever the hell he was, we sure whooped his ass!

He was a stupid, screwed-up teenager.

Out to beat us bloody for no reason. And we whooped his ass!

It was self-defense. Couldn't talk Old Nick out of him.
Lucky for him he run off.
Lucky for me.

Yeah. Well. Now—self-defense means common sense
like getting our ass down to the river for a wash-up.
While we're at it, Sis
we better scrub up
that blade.

∾　∾

(Knifebird: Urban slang for a creature similar to the Grim Reaper,
who appears to only the very old, and few survive the encounter.
Old Nick is Satan.)

QUEEN VICTORIA

This old house sat at Midway and Route One.

Old Fort Pierce beauty gone to rack and ruin.

Like Victorian mansions I seen in library books.

So, I called that house Victoria.

'Cause like Queen Victoria

      and most of us

she seen good times and bad.

We pulled boards off Victoria's back door

and shared the space

      with rats.

We?

That was me and Madge and sometime Sadie

but she likes the shelter when she can get it.

      Not me.

Me, I like to be free.

When I can.

      Free-free-free!

      Except in wicked weather.

And that's why I loved Victoria.

The queen kept a roof over our heads

like Mama did us kids

      like a chicken does her chicks.

Victoria shivered and wept tears

right along with us

but she kept us safe.

So we helped her think of better days

with Goodwill junk bin stuff

      not good enough for most folk

but to us, finery and make-do beds

and drapes across the boarded windows.

Made Victoria 'member when she was a lady.

Made it a real home for us ladies.

Sort of.

Soon come two near-grown boys one day,
following me and Madge and Sadie home
          like two stray pups.
I clutched the knife in my pocket.
Just in case.

Said they be watching us.

Said sleeping in a broke-down house
was better than under the I-95 bridge.
          Said we'd be safer together.

There was the white boy name of Cleroy
who ran away from foster care
because they *didn't* care.
He never knew his mama
and his daddy was killed in a drive-by
for cheatin' on a crack deal.

Jethro wished he had no mama.
His mama was a ho'
who passed him round to men
that liked little boys.
At twelve, he took the streets.
Never saw his mama again.

Anyway, they were OK boys to us.
	But they moved on
		when we ladies moved on.
And it wasn't by choice.

A big road-fixin' job rolled through
like a giant
and it broke Victoria's bones
and ground them down to powder.

Victoria's gone
long live the queen
in our memories.

CHANGE OF FORTUNE

Sadie set a tray of Big Macs and a Coke
on our table by the window
where we can look out and see trees
        just being quiet trees
watching everything that's going on
        just like Sadie and me.

Somebody's having hard times, I said.
Look here at this change.

How'd you get change?

I passed the time of day
with that little old lady
that was drinking coffee there.

Seems to me

she coulda used this change herself

but she folded it in my hand and said

> *Maggie, I know it don't look like much*

> *but good things come in small packages!*

When I looked up—*whoosh!*

She was out of sight, Sadie.

And here you come with Big Macs and a Coke.

> Now. Look at these.

Nobody spends old coins like this.

They keep it for their kids.

> Or their grands.

> *You lookin' a gift horse in the mouth, Maggie?*

No.

I just get a funny feeling sometimes.

Like an angel whispering in my ear.

> See here?

A silver dollar like Mama gave me once.

> Old Ben Franklin half-dollar

buffalo nickels

> Indian heads

nineteen-and-forty-three pennies

     one steel, couple copper.

     All I ever saw of them was steel ones.

Me, too.

Mama said pennies were made of steel that year

because copper helped the army

give Old Hitler what was coming to him!

     And

they took the nickel out of nickels, Sadie.

     Did you know that?

Nope. So why they still called nickels?

I don't know why they still call them nickels!

And I don't know these copper pennies are real!

     Look.

Blurry letters on the front of this one.

And you see Abe Lincoln over here?

     Why

it looks like he got an extra ear!

Yup. The better to hear you with!

She cackles like an old biddy.

> *And, yeah, the blurry one*
> *looks like penny-maker man*
> *was flying high when he went to work!*

She cackles again, fit to lay an egg.
Everybody looks around.
That sound just gets my hackles up.

Yeah, well. I said.
    Sadie
I got that funny feeling again.
Maybe the library lady will know if they're real.

DISEMBODIED TEETH

Monday morning at ten.
I'm on the bus
to the free dental clinic again.
Lady sat down next to me and smiled
and opened her magazine.

In there I saw an old set of false teeth
some good, some broke or cracked
or stained with wear and age
set in an ugly, dark-metal frame.

Now ain't that a sorry sight, I said.
I feel bad for whoever had to wear them.
We shook our heads at the pitiful sight,
and she looked at me with a soft, sad smile.

It's sad—she said—*the lies they tell—*
the things they ban from the history books
the tales they make themselves believe
so they can sleep at night. And

I'm angry to learn this in my old age.
She pointed to the page again.
It's like learning, when I was ten,
there really was no Santa Claus.

Because, when I was ten, I believed
Washington's teeth were made of wood.
Why wouldn't I believe my history book?
It was written by grownups much smarter than me!

From what I see there, I said, they don't look like wood.
They look more like ivory. Maybe. You know?
Like ivory piano keys yellow with age.
I'll bet that's it. What does it say?

Not ivory—she said, slow-shaking her head—*it says*
these teeth were pulled from the mouths of his slaves.

We both got very quiet for quite a while.

Well—I said—lookin' back, the best we can hope is

they was bad teeth pulled from slaves' heads.

Or maybe they pulled them from the dead?

Or maybe, Ol' George, he bought them, you know?

Rich folk coulda' bought real teeth back then.

      But

      I'm just thinkin' practical now

I sure wish somebody I knew could use

all the bad teeth I've got to lose.

      She smiled. *Why not try the Tooth Fairy?*

Huh.

Nope.

She's just a lie, too.

We ladies sat silent for the rest of the ride.

But I knew we old souls were tied somehow

by our anger for cruelty, deception, and lies.

SMELLING MEMORIES

August.

Florida.

That combo sends me

looking for shelter faster

than an Eskimo in a blizzard.

On my way to a meal at Helping Hands

I stop at a stand of deep piney trees

cooking

in the Florida sun.

Like burger in the fry pan.

Piney woods send a scent

just as sweet to my mind

as burger to my stomach do.

I recall Carolina piney woods
when first I married Webster.
Alex Adair Webster.
Oh, but he be enough
to fill a book of his own.
Go 'way, Webster.
Let me go on.

Seems that piney smell
wherever I be
drifts in
breathing the breath of life
into near-dead memories.

Sweet blood of the trees
calling out to me to flee, wild and free
into their deep, dark, waiting arms
where blessed coolness caresses a body
like
slow lovin'
on a perfect day.

Memories...

Of Alex.
Of Fox and Todd
our babies.

Memories...

That piney stand now stinks of sorrow.
Its arms, of a sudden
—too dark, too deep—
seem to whisper of final sleep.

That piney smell, like a lynch noose
chokes the breath right out of me,
yanks me back to a terrible time—

No more memories!
Better move along.
Helping Hands be filling up fast.

⌘　⌘　⌘

MORE THAN A BONY OLD BODY

From a distance

I couldn't tell which came first

up on Avenue H, in the bygones

     that rickety shotgun house or

     the lady standing up front in the driveway.

She stood clutching a walker

and scanning the street

waiting for somebody

or something.

I could see her eyeing me

as I pushed down the walk

past purple crepe myrtles

then under that wide-armed Poinciana tree
cut back by half since last I passed.

Of a sudden, she *yoo-hooed* me.
    I stopped.
    Looked up.
Didn't see her *looking down* on me
like some folks do.
Just a pruney old white-haired lady
in a sun-flowered housecoat
lime-colored slippers
and a smile 'most big as she was.

Beside her was two loaded wagons.
I swear I could hear them moaning
under boxes piled high with junk.
Then, with one leaf-dry hand a-flapping
Pruney waved me on up.
So I parked my cart on the grass
and went up to see what she wanted of me.

"Sister," said she, "My handyman failed
and as you see, I surely can't make it
down there with these.
          So
would you kindly take this trash
to roadside for me?"

Eye to eye, both of us knew
the only rule there be for harmony:
Do unto others as you would have them do unto you.

If I was that dried-up, bony old lady
I'd want a kindness done unto me.
          So
I trundled each one of those wagons down
though mightily they protested
          groaning and screeching
          Hey! Our wheels need greasing!
I piled up the trash and took a look-through.
Nothing there I could use.
I stopped, swiped my sweaty face
then toted each wagon back up.

Pruney clasped my hands real tight.

Though her hands felt like thin, dry sticks

her eyes were bright and alive

with a fearsome light.

"One good kindness deserves another," she said.

Take what my handyman doesn't deserve."

I stared at my clamped hands

       wondering

What on earth is this old lady thinking...?

       but

as they slowly unfolded

out sprung a ten and two twenties.

I heard the coo of a dove and a flutter of wings

      and when I looked up

         Pruney was gone.

I never saw her again

when I passed this way.

So, I believe I met an angel that day
or maybe God himself.

If I'd spent more time reading her eyes
instead of the skin she was in
        I'd have known that though Pruney
        might leave this earth soon,
        that spirit of love would go on.

COLOR ME UNDERSTANDING

I don't like those flower balls
on that bush.
They bloom dusty and pale
faded
like they dying aborning.
Ain't got the gumption
to bust out bright red
and make the world happier
not low down
with one more reminder
the Grim Reaper's on your tail.

If you want to catch my eye
bring me a smile
shining bright red
and dancing with
life!

Some folks don't like your color, Maggie.

Aw, Mama, flowers ain't people.
And I can dislike them if I so choose.

Plants have feelings.
They die
just like people
if you don't love and care for them.

Well, somebody's caring for them
so I can dislike them if I so choose.

Child
an open heart
soaks in water of life
and shares it freely.
A closed heart shrivels and dies.

Mama—it's a flower.

Maggie—it is one
with its Creator.

Okay.
You got me.
I'll let it be.

You will love it just as it is.
As your Creator loves you.

Yes, Mama.
I'll remember.

❧　❧

INGENUITY

Rain made this bench soppin' wet

so I just wiped it down

with newspaper out the garbage can.

     Gotta set a spell.

These boots Lillian gave me

     when I got caught on a day like this

     outside her Salvation Army store

these boots Lillian gave me

     look at them!

Covered with mud like chocolate icing!

That lady goin' by now
staring scared-like at me
laughing to myself
        like I'm a crazy lady
well
        maybe
but my chocolate-icing-cupcake boots
puts me in mind of my cousin Barbie-Mae
four or five years old, just like me
when we played in her backyard
in Clewiston.

Barbie-Mae wanted to bake
some mud cakes and mudpies
            but
Auntie Eliza said no to some water
'cause later we'd all go to town.

Barbie-Mae came out with a scowl on her face
and her eyes switchin' left-right-left-right
like they done when she was thinking.

"Don't wanna go to town," says she

and she pulled down her panties and peed

right

     in

         the dirt

which was okay with me

    so I did too

    and we made enough mud food

    to feed all the folks in town.

When Auntie and Mama found out

we thought-no doubt-we'd get whipped

    but Auntie and Mama

    just laughed till they cried

and couldn't squeeze out any more.

Then stiflin' their giggles

praised our *in-gin-noo-ity*

but said not to do it again.

✍   ✎

MISS KATEY

Old Miss Katey
was the whitest white lady
I ever did see.
White of skin
and pure white within.

She never saw me
more or less than I am.
Just like I saw her
the good woman within
under the skin.

She lived in Fort Pierce
all her ninety-five years
calm in the raging storm
touching all as it sweeps by
bearing changes and strife.

Miss Katey was a butterfly

in the garden of life

with all its wonders and weevils.

She fluttered lightly 'mid bustlin' bees

seeing what they never did see.

And while she lay to the end in peace

at the service at Gateway Hill

I could hear my very dear friend say

Follow your heart, and 'Do unto others....'

for all are your needy sisters and brothers.

Miss Katey

they say it's never too late.

So.

Maybe before I pass through, like you

there's a way for me to give back.

For I been *done unto* in ways good and bad,

and all my travels hold learnin's to be had.

OLD YEAR, NEW YEAR

Old Year, New Year
all the same

the way I see it

The world turns
and we say the sun rises
on a new day
       while we know it don't.

Just illusion
just a story we tell ourselves
to make us believe
       we be the center of everything.

But we just a speck
in the eye of God

And sometimes
we probably feel to him
like a big, old splinter in that eye
        for all we do unto each other.

Maybe that's why it feels
like he's moved on
to create something better
which is why
        so much is
                what it is.

Still
every once in awhile
when I seems to need it most
I find he's left behind
an abundance of
        angels in human skin.

And then I think

that old boy still got his eye on us

and maybe New Year

        won't be as bad as Old Year.

And maybe

he just be waiting

for our prodigal minds

to come home and see

he's still

the center of everything.

HOW I SEE IT

Seems like today

too many folks go their own way

thinkin' they the only ones

that know anything.

Thinkin' there ain't no sense

in sharing and caring for others

cause it don't benefit them.

How I see it is

If all you got is   your   stuff

If all you got is   your   color

If all you got is   your   religion

If all you got is   your   team

If all you got is what you've been told

and not the truth you dug up on your own

       it don't make you better than anyone else

       it just makes you dumber for thinkin' so.

We turnin' inside ourselves

instead of reaching out hereabouts.

I remember many of our best days.

       And strange as it sounds

       some of our best days

       came bound in with the worst

       and shook us awake to who we were.

       Like World War Two.

I was too little to remember

but Mama told me story after story about

       food being rationed across the nation

       and nobody howled *poor me.*

They turned patches of grass into Victory Gardens

and hardened themselves to win.

       It wasn't a time to throw things away.

       Folks mended and fixed them, used them, made do.

They recycled fat—rags—paper—silk—string—
metal—rubber—nylon—and many other things
        to settle the devil's hash
        and end that awful war!

And there's so much more, child.
        That's what books are for.

Maybe the trials we going through now
is our time's World War Two.
I guess folks gotta decide
        Do we pull together as one
        or let them
                pull us apart
                one
                        by
                                one?

ABOUT THE AUTHOR

Virginia Nygard

Award-winning author in multiple genres for
multiple years.

Member Florida Writers Association

FWA Regional Director 2015-2020

Treasure Coast Writers Group Leader 2010-2019

Royal Palm Literary Awards

National League of American Pen Women
Vero Beach, Florida Branch past Vice President

Member Florida State Poets Association

Follow Virginia's blog:
www.dialogondialogue.wordpress.com

Follow on Facebook:
www.facebook.com/virginia.nygard

Contact the author at:
nygardv@comcast. net

"If my doctor told me I had only six minutes to live... I'd
type a little faster." - Isaac Asimov